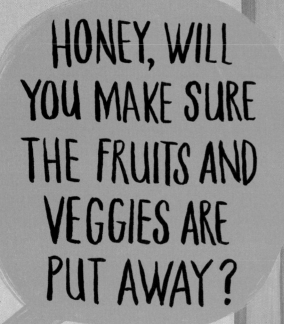

HONEY, WILL YOU MAKE SURE THE FRUITS AND VEGGIES ARE PUT AWAY?

SURE, MOM!

THIS IS A BORZOI BOOK PUBLISHED BY ALFRED A. KNOPF

Copyright © 2018 by Mark Hoffmann

All rights reserved. Published in the United States by Alfred A. Knopf, an imprint of Random House Children's Books, a division of Penguin Random House LLC, New York.

Knopf, Borzoi Books, and the colophon are registered trademarks of Penguin Random House LLC.

Visit us on the Web! rhcbooks.com

Educators and librarians, for a variety of teaching tools, visit us at RHTeachersLibrarians.com

Library of Congress Cataloging-in-Publication Data is available upon request. ISBN 978-1-5247-1991-3 (trade) — ISBN 978-1-5247-1992-0 (lib. bdg.) — ISBN 978-1-5247-1993-7 (ebook)

The text of this book was hand-lettered by the artist.

The illustrations were made using gouache with digital compositing (and a little help from a special tomato).

MANUFACTURED IN CHINA
June 2018
10 9 8 7 6 5 4 3 2 1
First Edition

FOR MY PARENTS, WHO ARE BOTH BANANAS

FRUIT BOWL

MARK HOFFMANN

Alfred A. Knopf
New York

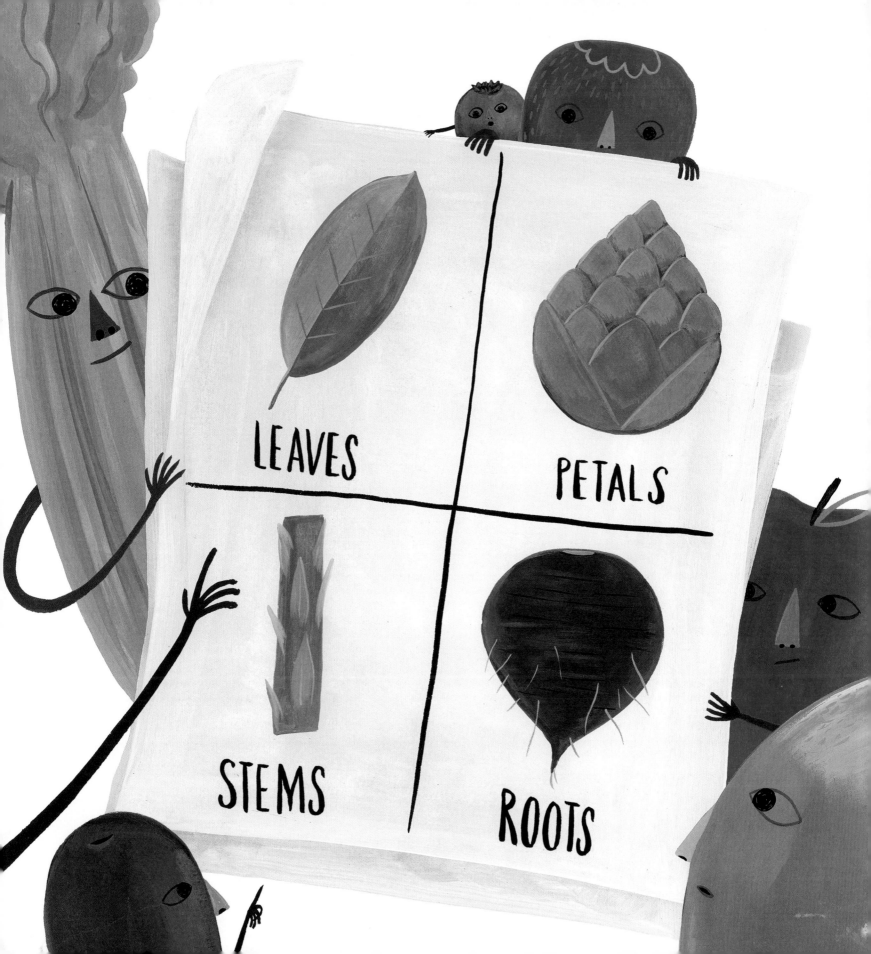

LEAVES

PETALS

STEMS

ROOTS

...AND LOOK AT THIS.
N2150 | 9776 | LPH
52913CBH | X-RAY 1-76
PATIENT: TOM B. ATO
FOR OFFICE USE ONLY
OH, ARE YOU ALL RIGHT?
THOSE SPOTS? THOSE ARE MY SEEDS. IT'S HOW WE MAKE MORE FRUITS.

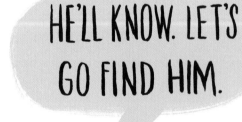

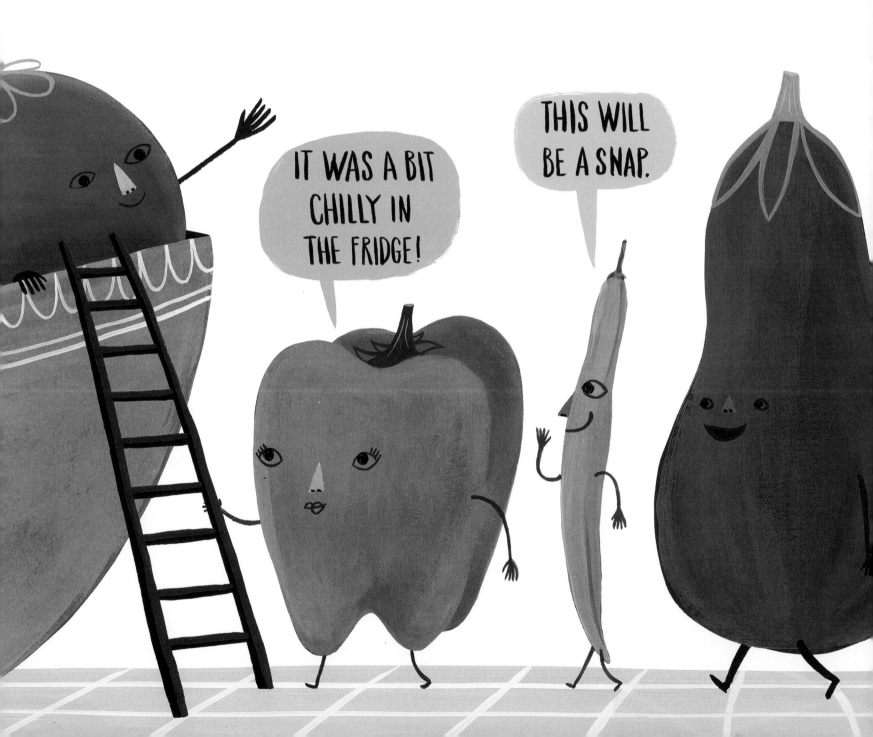